Trash Heap Trisha

Copyright Stuff
because... legal

Dedicated to graphic designers, especially my sister

Adina Warshawsky

You guys are the unsung heroes
of the literary world.

...And probably a bunch of other worlds too.

Thank you for teaching me how to use InDesign
so I could stop calling you every five minutes.

...Now I only call every seven.

Behold a random font about which you surely harbor many opinions.

Trash Heap Trisha has three kids
And Tupperware with random lids.
She thinks "one day" she'll sort 'em out,
But why do **that** when she can **pout**?

Yaaaaay TRISHA!

Tra-Trash Heap Trisha – YAY!!

Trash Heap Trisha understands
When God laughs at her far-fetched plans.
"Be on time today?" --**Guffaw!**
She laughs with God. "Good one - haha!"

Yaaaaay TRISHA!

Tra-Trash Heap Trisha - YAY!!

Trash Heap Trisha calls in sick.
She's running late; she's thinking quick.
"Cough! Cough!" she coughs. Her boss says "Fine!"
And Trisha loses overtime.

Awwwwww TRISHA!

Tra-Trash Heap Trisha - Aww!!

Trash Heap Trisha swats at flies.
Her sink is piled to the skies.
She ponders her disgusting fate,
And starts to scrub a grungy plate.

Yaaaaay TRISHA!

Tra-Trash Heap Trisha – YAY!!

Trash Heap Trisha's had enough.
Washing dishes is too tough.
What a stinky, smelly quandry--
"Wait!" she cries, "I'll do the laundry!"

Yeeaaah TRISHA?

Tra-Trash Heap Trisha - WILL YOU?

Trash Heap Trisha knows the sun
Will set before her work is done.
She sets the laundry on the floor.
That's what the **Biggest Shelf** is for!

Ohhhhhh TRISHA!

Tra-Trash Heap Trisha – Oh!!

Trash Heap Trisha shops online.
She'll clean her house some other time.
Right now she needs a Snark-O-Pad.
The kind she saw once in that ad...

Yaaaaay TRISHA!

Tra-Trash Heap Trisha – SCORE!!

Trash Heap Trisha gets the mail.
Snark-O-Pad was **such** a fail!
Neither snark nor flatteries,
And didn't come with batteries!

Awwwwww TRISHA!

Tra-Trash Heap Trisha - Aww!!

Trash Heap Trisha knows the drill.
She battles with an iron will.
She'll take 'em down if they dare say,
"I'm sorry, ma'am, you feel that way..."

Awwwwww TRISHA!

Tra-Trash Heap Trisha - Aww!!

Trash Heap Trisha comes up short
When calling customer support.
She's out ten bucks, but she's not through –
She'll write a "really bad" review!

Ummmmm TRISHA?

Tra-Trash Heap Trisha – Why?

Trash Heap Trisha gives one star.
She hates the core of who they are!
She would give zero, if she could.
That one star's made of rotting wood.

Trash Heap Trisha's eyebrows furrow.
Stupid Better Business Bureau!
How dare they not take her side.
It seems that decency has died.

Awwwwww decency!

Tra-Trash Heap Trisha's - DECENCY!!

Trash Heap Trisha holds a grudge
Against the dumb small claims court Judge!
She lost her money and her case
But it's not over, Judgey Face!

Nooooo TRISHA!

Tra-Trash Heap Trisha - NO!!

Trash Heap Trisha's in contempt.
(She also **isn't** tax-exempt...)
She wracks up charges, but won't stop.
She's **livid** at that one-star shop!

Yiiiiikes TRISHA!

Tra-Trash Heap Trisha – STOP!!

Trash Heap Trisha's day's the pits
Because she couldn't call it quits.
"Use your powers for the good,"
Her mother always said she should.

Yaaaaaay TRISHA'S MOM!

Tra-Trash Heap Trisha's MOM!!

Trash Heap Trisha's on the run.
She hated gym, but this is fun.
She might evade the cops, but then
Tomorrow she must run again!

Nooooooo TRISHA!

Tra-Trash Heap Trisha - NO!!

Trash Heap Trisha gives a hiss.
She really wasn't built for this!
The slowest felon in the nation
Turns herself in to the station.

Yaaaaay TRISHA!

Tra-Trash Heap Trisha - YAY!!

Trash Heap Trisha has no bail,
So she sits alone in jail.
She gets a gift from husband Chad.
Oh, look at that – her Snark-O-Pad!

Awwwww TRISHA!

Tra-Trash Heap Trisha – Aww!!

Trash Heap Trisha makes it back
In time to eat a midnight snack.
Eventually she'll face the court,
But **this** time she'll keep comments short.

Yaaaaay TRISHA!

Tra-Trash Heap Trisha – YAY!!

Trash Heap Trisha learned her lesson,
Watched each word and face expression.
She bit her tongue and didn't pout.
The case against her got thrown out!

Yaaaaay TRISHA!

Tra-Trash Heap Trisha - YAY!!

Trash Heap Trisha still got fired.
That's okay, though. She is tired.
Now the house reeks of manure.
It's nothing that a nap won't cure!

Ummmmmm TRISHA?

Tra-Trash Heap Trisha - Umm??

Trash Heap Trisha sleeps it off,
And wakes up with a **real** cough!
She calls her old boss real quick
'Cause this time she's "for real" sick!

Huuuuuh TRISHA?

Tra-Trash Heap Trisha – Huh??

Trash Heap Trisha folds her clothes
While watching all her favorite shows.
She buys new dishes, scrubs the kitchen,
Gets her husband Chad to pitch in...

Yaaaaaay CHAD!

It's–it's about time – CHAD!!

Trash Heap Trisha looks around her.
Once again the mess has found her!
This, she thinks, *is why I don't.*
*I **hate** to clean, and now I **won't**!*

Truuuue TRISHA!

Tra-Trash Heap Trisha – TRUTH!!

Trash Heap Trisha reads a book,
And gives each of her kids **The Look.**
They make the house shine like a gem.
'Cause they know what is good for them!

Gooooo**oo TRISHA!**

Tra-Trash Heap Trisha – **YES!!**

Trash Heap Trisha still has dishes,
Laundry, and a million wishes.
Still has kids and husband Chad.
But she chucked the Snark-O-Pad!

Yaaaaay TRISHA!

Tra-Trash Heap Trisha - YAY!!

* ABOUT STORYTIME MOMMY *

We're a wacky bunch who embrace our quirks and the
remaining shreds of our sanity.

Join the Circle of Chaos at StorytimeMommy.com

Find us on YouTube by searching "Storytime Mommy"

Say hi at StorytimeMommy@gmail.com

We're good people! And also fun (at least we think so!) Say hi!

Legit, say hello!

StorytimeMommy@gmail.com